AuthorHouse™
1663 Liberty Drive
Bloomington, IN 47403
www.authorhouse.com
Phone: 833-262-8899

Because of the dynamic nature of the Internet, any web addresses or links contained in this book may have changed
since publication and may no longer be valid. The views expressed in this work are solely those of the author and do
not necessarily reflect the views of the publisher, and the publisher hereby disclaims any responsibility for them.

Author: Cyd Eisner
Book Design: Lamya Shawki El-Shacke

This book is printed on acid-free paper.

ISBN: 978-1-4817-2824-9 (sc)
978-1-4817-2825-6 (e)

Library of Congress Control Number: 2013904739

Print information available on the last page.

Published by AuthorHouse 01/20/2021

authorHOUSE®

SWALLOWED ALIVE

The Story of
Prophet Yunus (AS)
and The Whale

As told by Cyd Eisner

*This book is dedicated to my beautiful and precious daughters,
Rahma, Taqwa, Cyba, Moshira and Safia.*

*Narrated Abdullah ibn Abbas: If anyone continually asks pardon,
Allah will appoint for him a way out of every distress, and a relief from
every anxiety, and will provide for him from where he did not reckon.
[Abu Dawud Book 8, Number 1513]*

In the Name of Allah, the Most Gracious, the Most Merciful

Introduction

To all the Muslim children and non-Muslim children who read this story about Yunus (AS) or any of the stories about the Prophets, may you be inspired to follow their righteous and well-mannered example. May you also be inspired to make a difference in uniting the Muslim Ummah (nation) and to encourage peace throughout the world Insha'Allah (God Willing).

In the Islamic religion, Allah (SWT) is the Arabic and Islamic name for God, and Muslims believe that Allah (SWT) does exist. He sees and hears all that we do. Yunus's (AS) story is an excellent example. In Islam, all Allah's (SWT) creations: plants, animals, trees, etc. pray to Allah (SWT) in their own way and bow to Him in prayer.

On the Day of Judgment, all His creation will be witnesses regarding what we have done in this life and how we did it. Muslims believe that actions in this life determine if we will be accepted into paradise. Our tongues are going to tell Allah (SWT) how and what we spoke of in this life – was it done truthfully, respectfully, and kindly? Or did we use our voices to lie, hurt, gossip, and complain? Our eyes will reflect everything they witnessed, good or bad. Our hands will be a testament as to what they have touched or how we used them, good or evil. The ground will witness on our behalf, every area where we pray whether it is the corner of a room or out in some meadow – will be a witness to the bowing down to Him in praise. And on the last day, the earth will report all that happened, and then everyone will be shown their Book of Deeds.

Every creation submits to Allah (SWT) and even though we might not see them praying, that is considered the unseen and we must believe in the unseen. We can't see the air, but we know that it is there because we breathe it. We don't need to see an artist next to his painting to know he painted it. It is the same with Allah (SWT). You see His sky, stars, vast landscapes, bodies of water, insects, and animals. We can't physically see Allah (SWT), but we see Him through His creation – and we believe this is proof of His existence.

To become familiar with the Arabic terminology and acronyms used throughout this book, please refer to the glossary at the end of the story.

And lastly, thank you to my editor, W.E. Kinne and to my designer, Lamya El-Shacke; without you, this book would not be possible.

Cyd Eisner

The story begins in Nineveh (now known as Mosul, Iraq), the capitol of the Assyrian Empire, sometime around 800 B.C. With approximately 120,000 citizens, Nineveh was a beautiful land that flourished in trade, productivity, and wealth.

Despite the town's many blessings, these citizens displayed extreme immoral behavior – they lied, stole, and mistreated one another. Most importantly, they were worshiping idols instead of worshiping Allah (SWT) The One True God. Displeased with their behavior, Allah (SWT) decided to choose a very righteous citizen of Nineveh to speak to the people about their wrong doings – and He chose Yunus (AS).

Why was Yunus (AS) chosen? From birth, Allah (SWT) protected Yunus (AS) from participating in immoral and sinful behavior. Allah (SWT) protected all His Prophets in this manner. Allah (SWT) did this so when the time would come for these individuals to become prophets, they would be righteous and pure of heart, and able to teach and inspire others. However, until Allah (SWT) would actually *speak* to them through the Angel Jibreel (AS), these chosen few would not know the identity of their god.

Muslims believe that all human beings are born with a natural instinct to worship one god. However, as these children grow older, their parents teach them to follow _their_ ways and beliefs, like worshiping many gods. Eventually, everyone in Nineveh learned to worship idols and multiple gods. Yunus (AS) was the one exception. But he did not judge his people; he continued believing in one god and living each day as lawfully and respectfully as possible.

Little did he know that someday, Allah (SWT) would choose him to become a Prophet and deliver a message to his fellow citizens. Imagine his surprise when he received the Call from Allah (SWT)!

One day, Allah (SWT) sent the Angel Jibreel (AS) to appear before Yunus (AS). Jibreel (AS) told Yunus (AS) he must speak to the people of Nineveh at once, and get them to stop praying to their idols and false gods. The Angel said Nineveh would be destroyed and the people would suffer if they did not agree to stop their corrupt and immoral ways. Jibreel (AS) instructed Yunus (AS) to teach the people how to worship The One True God and guide them as they begin living more righteous lives.

Wanting to please Allah (SWT), Yunus (AS) began his challenging task. For several days, he closely observed the actions of his people. What he witnessed was horrible – people worshiping idols, stealing and cheating one another, and more. As he watched them, everything became clear to Yunus (AS), and he now understood why Allah (SWT) wanted him to speak to the people. Strong and disciplined, Yunus (AS) chose to live a righteous life and not give in to temptation. But the people of Nineveh appeared to be easily tempted by sin, and he knew they needed his help and guidance.

So the next morning, Yunus (AS) stood on top of a tree stump so everyone could see and hear him, and he addressed the people: "Men, women and children of Nineveh, I am a Prophet of The One True God (Allah (SWT)). I am here at Allah's (SWT) command, to tell you to stop your sinful and impure ways and teach you how to worship Him, instead of your idols. There is One True God Allah (SWT), and you must learn to worship only Him. Heed my warning: If you do not put an end to the worshiping of other gods, you will experience the powerful wrath of Allah (SWT) – and it will be a sight *unimaginable*."

Day after day, Yunus (AS) stood on top of the tree stump and spoke to the people, trying to get them to listen and start changing their ways. He continued to warn them about the wrath of Allah (SWT). But the people ignored him and went about their business.

Then one day while Yunus (AS) was delivering his

message, a man stepped onto the tree stump and stood next to Yunus (AS). The man began shouting at Yunus (AS). "I really do not care *who* you are mister, or what your purpose might be! I suggest you leave and find some other people to preach to! We are not interested in what you have to say!"

Several people started to approach the tree stump, and Yunus (AS) could tell by their expressions they were angry and annoyed. One man threatened, "Yunus (AS)! We have heard enough of your ridiculous preaching and warnings! Leave Nineveh peacefully or we will _force_ you out!" A crowd

quickly gathered around Yunus (AS). These people agreed with the others that Yunus (AS) should leave. However, instead of leaving, Yunus (AS) jumped off the tree stump, planted his feet firmly on the ground, stood up straight, and held his head up. He knew his words would be met with opposition, but he was prepared to carry out Allah's (SWT) command.

Yunus (AS) took a deep breath and boldly spoke to the

crowd for the last time, "Citizens of Nineveh, Allah (SWT) has instructed me to warn you of your immoral behavior. The love and devotion to your false gods _must_ _stop_ or all of Nineveh will be destroyed! Allah (SWT) will show no mercy."

The people called him a liar and mocked him. "Let it happen," they told Yunus (AS). Then several people started pushing him. Some even picked up rocks and sticks to beat him. Yunus (AS) shouted, "Stop! If this is how you want to live your lives, then so be it. I will leave you to your misery." Feeling furious and discouraged, Yunus (AS) turned and walked away.

As soon as Yunus (AS) began to leave, the people of Nineveh cheered triumphantly. Almost immediately – the sky became dark, obscured by thick, enraged-looking clouds. Lightning bolts lit up the sky and began striking everything in their path, and the ground was trembling violently! Balls of fire began falling from the sky creating large craters as they hit the ground!

The people were _terrified_. As they stood there, clinging to one another and watching in horror, they remembered the people of 'Ad, Thamud and Nuh (Noah) (AS). They recalled how Allah (SWT) destroyed them in a blink of an eye. They definitely did not want the same fate. So all the men, women, and children bowed down in shame calling out to Allah (SWT), The One True God, and asked for His Forgiveness and Mercy.

As faith started to penetrate the hearts of the people, the dark clouds began to disappear, the earth stopped trembling, and the sky became clear again. Hearing their prayers for forgiveness and mercy, Allah (SWT) ended His Wrath and forgave the people, blessing them once again. After thanking Allah (SWT) for His Mercy, the people prayed for Yunus (AS) to return and guide them in their daily lives.

Meanwhile, Yunus (AS) boarded a ship in hopes of finding his way and place in the world. He felt frustrated and angry because the people of Nineveh chose not to accept his message from Allah (SWT), nor did they want to start believing in The One True God. Instead, they ridiculed him; and having had enough of their anger and ignorance, he allowed the people to force him out of Nineveh. Trying to put that experience out of his mind, Yunus (AS) looked out at the water and was pleased at how calm and peaceful the sea looked. The sunlight sparkled on the gentle waves. It was a beautiful sight.

Shortly after sundown, the ship's passengers began to feel anxious due to an eerie stillness in the air. Black clouds began covering the sky, and suddenly the air became cold and the wind picked up violently, lightning filled the sky and thunderous roars could be heard, putting a chill in the hearts of the ship's passengers. No longer calm and peaceful, the sea became violent as large waves appeared and began crashing against the ship, tossing it about like a small toy.

The crew and passengers aboard the ship feared for their safety and immediately began praying to several gods for help. The captain was convinced that the god of the sea was infuriated. "Too much water is seeping into the ship; we must lighten the load," said the captain. So the crew, with Yunus (AS) helping them, started throwing equipment, baggage, and just about everything overboard. One crew member said, "The ship is still too heavy! I think one of us must leave and jump into the sea, to save the ship and everyone aboard!"

For that reason, they decided to draw names. So they quickly wrote down the names of the ship's crew members and passengers. The captain would randomly pick a name, and that person would have to jump into the sea. The name drawn was *Yunus* (AS). However, the people knew Yunus (AS) was a hardworking, honorable man so they decided to draw again. While they were drawing names for a second time, Yunus (AS) turned his thoughts to Allah (SWT). Yunus (AS) knew he left the town of Nineveh without Allah's (SWT) permission. The people needed guidance, but he lost faith in them and in himself, and he walked away. But most importantly, Yunus (AS) knew he should have trusted Allah (SWT) to help him successfully guide the people of Nineveh. He knew it was *his* turn to be punished and now he must accept his fate. Another name was drawn – Yunus (AS) was selected *again*! Surprised, the captain and the others looked at each other, wondering what they should do. Why must Yunus (AS), such a decent man, end his life at sea? But without hesitation, Yunus (AS) bravely walked over to the edge of the ship and, as he called out Allah's (SWT) name, he courageously jumped into the roaring sea.

Disappearing under the enraged waves, Yunus (AS) finally floated to the surface gasping for air. Treading for his life, he noticed a massive whale coming straight

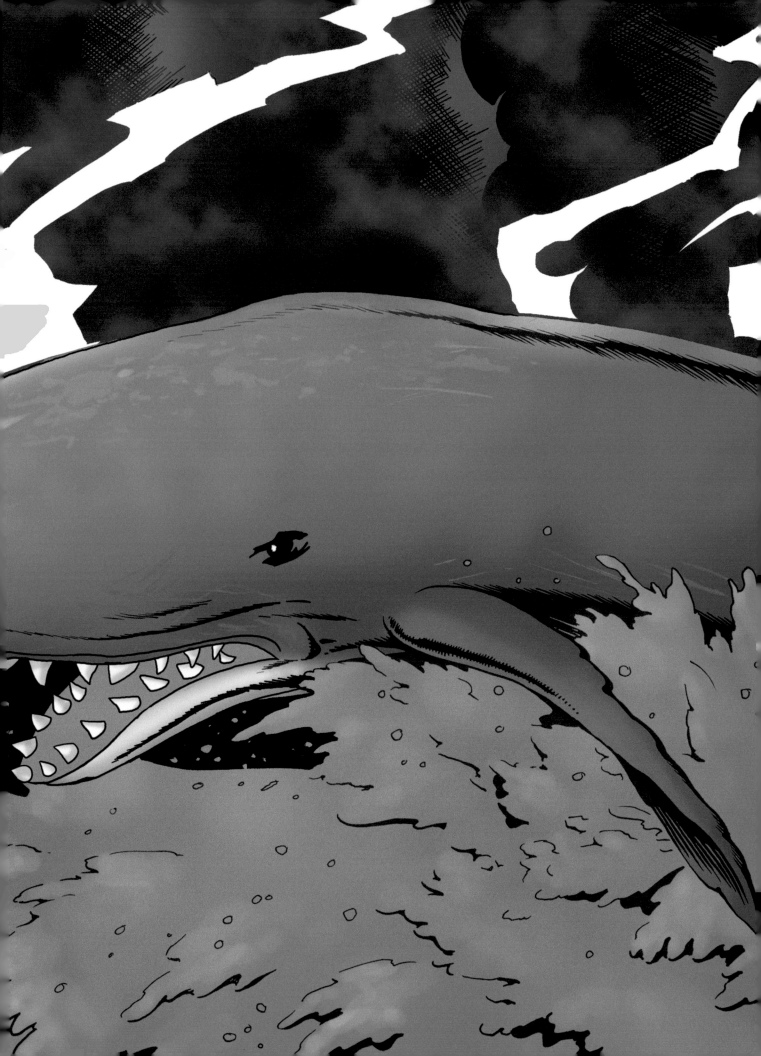

towards him. Yunus (AS) put all his strength and effort into swimming away from the whale, but something was terribly wrong. It felt like the sea's current had changed direction and he was trying to push through a *stone wall*. Yunus (AS) had become a prisoner of the sea. It was as if Allah (SWT) had commanded the waves to "chain and shackle" him to the sea's fury. As the whale approached, Yunus (AS) decided to courageously accept his fate.

The monstrous creature came closer and opened its mouth, revealing its terrifyingly large, jagged teeth. Surely, Yunus (AS) must have thought he was going to die! Then the whale scooped up Yunus (AS) with its enormous mouth, and swallowed him *whole*. In he went, down to the dark abyss of the mammal's belly. Expecting to die as the whale swallowed him, Yunus (AS) was surprised to discover he was still alive, and still in one piece. However, he was also aware of the uncertainty facing him. He went from being a prisoner of the sea to being violently thrown into a world of darkness and isolation inside the belly of a whale!

Most people, if swallowed by a whale and plunged into darkness, would probably panic and feel anxious. But Yunus (AS) was no ordinary man; he was now a Prophet, chosen by Allah (SWT), and therefore displayed immense inner strength. To ease his mind and remain calm, Yunus (AS) began softly speaking Allah's (SWT) name, over and over. Then suddenly, he found himself saying: *"There is no god but You (O Lord). Glory be to You. Verily I was of the unjust."* [1]

---

[1] *The Qur'an, Surah 21: 87*

Yunus (AS) was repenting because he realized he made a *terrible* mistake when he walked away from the people of Nineveh. Even though the people were rude and mean to him, Yunus (AS) knew he should have stayed in Nineveh and completed his mission, as commanded by Allah (SWT). He repeated this dua'a (a supplication for forgiveness) numerous times, in hopes Allah (SWT) would hear him and forgive him.

Every sea creature could hear Yunus's (AS) voice praying to Allah (SWT) from inside a place incomprehensible to humans – *the belly of a whale!* The creatures encircled the whale to celebrate the praises of Allah (SWT) in their own unique way. Allah (SWT) watched and listened as Yunus (AS) sincerely repented and asked for His Forgiveness.

Allah (SWT) commanded the whale to spit out Yunus (AS) onto an island. Without hesitation, the whale did what it was commanded to do. Its massive, robust body rose out of the sea and spewed Yunus (AS) with enough force to land him on the soft sands of an island.

Although he had no broken bones or serious injuries, Yunus (AS) was aware that his skin was severely burned from the whale's stomach acids. When the sun's scorching rays first touched his wounded skin, he cried out in agony. But Yunus (AS) decided to ignore the pain and continue supplicating, because his love for Allah (SWT) was more powerful than any type of distress he would ever endure.

As Yunus (AS) prayed, a gourd vine miraculously appeared and began sprouting multiple branches. It grew into a tall, large arch, full enough to shade him from the sun's rays. Then by Allah's (SWT) Will, He healed Yunus

(AS) and forgave him for his disobedience. Yunus (AS) would have remained inside the whale's belly until the Day of Judgment, had it not been for his repentance and love for Allah (SWT).

Allah (SWT) said, "And indeed, Jonah (Yunus in Arabic) (AS) was among the messengers. When he ran away to the laden ship. And he drew lots and was among the losers. Then the fish swallowed him, while he was blameworthy. And had he not been of those who exalt Allah. He would have remained inside its belly until the Day they are resurrected. But We threw him onto the open shore while he was ill. And We caused to grow over him a gourd vine. And We sent him to [his people of] a hundred thousand or more. And they believed, so We gave them enjoyment [of life] for a time."²

---

² *The Qur'an, Surah 37: 139-148*

Once Yunus (AS) recovered his strength and his skin healed completely, Allah (SWT) instructed him to return to Nineveh and guide the people to a better way of life and worship. When Yunus (AS) arrived in Nineveh, he received a warm welcome from the people – they were so happy to see him again! They told Yunus (AS) they were ready to listen to him, and they wanted to become good, honorable people. They promised to dispose of their idols and begin worshiping The One True God (Allah (SWT)). *"How wonderful,"* thought Yunus (AS) as he raised his hands to his face, thanking Allah (SWT) for His Mercy, His Forgiveness, and His Blessings. And so, Yunus (AS) stayed in Nineveh, helping his people live better lives and teaching them how to glorify The One True God (Allah (SWT)). Yunus (AS) succeeded in his mission to get all the people to practice *monotheism*, the worshiping of one God. And this pleased Allah (SWT) greatly.

To all of you who just read this story, I ask you to please always remember Allah (SWT) and He will remember you. Love Allah (SWT) and He will love you. Put your trust in Allah (SWT), and He will provide you with faith and courage. Narrated Abdullah ibn Abbas: If anyone continually asks pardon, Allah will appoint for him a way out of every distress, and a relief from every anxiety, and will provide for him from where he did not reckon. [Abu Dawud Book 8, Number 1513]

Glossary

Abu Dawud Book 8, Number 1513: This is one of nine books of authentic Hadith, which are narration's concerning the words and deeds of Prophet Muhammad (SAW) or traditions. Hadith are regarded by traditional Islamic schools of jurisprudence as important tools for understanding the Qur'an and in most matters jurisprudence.

Allah (SWT): is the Arabic and Islamic name for God.

Angel Jibreel (AS): is the Arabic and Islamic name for the biblical name Archangel Gabriel (AS).

AS: spelled out in English transliteration, "Alayhi al-salam" means peace and blessings upon him. This is the expression said after saying the names of all the Prophets and Angels. One can either say AS or SAW after saying the names of the Prophets. The expression that should be said after saying the names of the Angels is AS not SAW. A Muslim should say this out of respect for them and to display proper etiquette.

Dua'a: means supplication, an action in which Muslims ask Allah (SWT) to provide ourselves or someone else with something good or beneficial.

Insha'Allah: means God Willing.

Nuh (AS): is the Arabic and Islamic name for the biblical name Prophet Noah (AS).

SAW: spelled out in English transliteration, "Sall Allahu alay-hi-wa-salam" means may Allah (SWT) honor him and grant him peace. This is the expression said after saying the names of all the Prophets. One can say AS or SAW. SAW is primarily said after saying Prophet Muhammad's (SAW) name because he is the last and final prophet and because of a certain verse in the Qur'an that is mentioned specifically for only him. "Verily God and His angels bless the Prophet! O you who believe, send blessings unto him and greet him with a salutation worthy of respect." [3] Muslims should say this out of respect for them and to display proper etiquette.

SWT: spelled out in the English transliteration, "Subhanahu wa ta'ala" means Glorified and Exalted is He. This is the expression said after saying Allah's (God's) name. A Muslim should say this out of respect for Allah (SWT) and to display proper etiquette for the Almighty.

Qur'an: is the last revelation to mankind sent to Prophet Muhammad (SAW). Also known as the miracle of Prophet Muhammad (SAW). The Holy Qur'an is still to this day in its original form and protected by Allah (SWT).

Yunus (AS): is the Arabic and Islamic name for the biblical name Jonah (AS).

Ummah: means the Muslim nation.

---

[3] *The Quran, Surah 33: 56*

About the Author

Cyd Eisner recently began writing books for Muslim children of all ages and for children of all faiths in an effort to encourage better understanding and to cultivate an appreciation of the Islamic religion. Cyd converted from Judaism to Islam in 1999. She received her B.A. from the University of Hartford in 2004, and she now lives in Virginia with her husband and five children.

Printed in the United States
By Bookmasters